A GIFT OF A RAINBOW

stories by
the Students of
Laurel Elementary School

illustrations by
Vuthy Kuon

PROVIDENCE PUBLISHING COMPANY

Whether physical or emotional,
we weather different kinds of storms in our lives as children,
as well as adults.
Our desire through these writings is to instill hope in those who are in despair
and to let them know that in the darkest hour of their lives,
after every storm,
a rainbow will appear offering hope and the promise of a new tomorrow.

EDITED BY DENNIS DEVORICK

Text copyright © 2006 by Laurel Elementary School
Illustrations copyright © 2006 by Vuthy Kuon
All rights reserved.
Published by
PROVIDENCE PUBLISHING COMPANY
www.providencepublishing.com
(888) 966-3833
Printed in China
First Printing 10 9 8 7 6 5 4 3 2

———————————

Library of Congress Catalog Card Number 2005911416
A Gift of a Rainbow / Vuthy Kuon
Summary: A collection of poems and short stories
written by students in grades K-6
at Laurel Elementary School in New Castle, Pennsylvania.
ISBN 0-9753004-4-x

TABLE OF CONTENTS

This book is dedicated to
Debbie Bakewell-McEwen

Have you ever noticed how mesmerized we become when looking at a rainbow? Its colors are so beautiful majestic, miraculous and heavenly. When a rainbow appears you can see people, young and old, gathered with fingers pointing toward the sky in awesome wonder as they enjoy a few moments of free entertainment together. It's almost as they've entered an art museum with free admission, to view the "most talked about" painting featured.

We, the teachers and students of Laurel Elementary, had the unforgettable privilege to view a rainbow like no other. Its rays shined over our school playground during recess on December 14, 1994.

What made this rainbow so miraculous? Well, it hadn't rained all day and yet a rainbow chose to appear over our playground just when we needed it most. What made it so beautiful and majestic? It was so unexpected and so welcomed, more than ever. We knew it was a gift that spread not only over the swing sets, but also into the hearts, minds and souls of everyone viewing it.

What made it so heavenly? We believe it was a priceless gift, heaven sent, by our beloved teacher and friend, Debbie Bakewell-McEwen, who had celebrated her earthly death the night before the rainbow appeared. We believe it was "Debbie's Masterpiece."

Only Debbie could find the perfect sign to help ease our sorrow. She knew it would take something as beautiful, majestic, miraculous and heavenly as a rainbow to comfort us. We believe it was Debbie's way of letting us know that she was happy. If you knew our friend, you would agree that this rainbow was undeniably Debbie, a true masterpiece.

The group that gathered to view the rainbow on December 14th will always remember that as rainbows go on forever, so will the spirit of Debbie Bakewell-McEwen. We dedicate this book to you and your rainbow.

A New Box of Crayons
by Kindergartners

I have a new box of crayons.

The red one reminds me of a stop sign, cherries and a ladybug.

The orange one reminds me of pumpkin pie, a basketball and fire.

The yellow one reminds me of a bus, a banana and a bumble bee.

The green one reminds me of a Christmas tree, broccoli and pickles.

The blue one reminds me of rain, blueberries and toothpaste.

The indigo one reminds me of jeans, blackberries and shadows.

The violet one reminds me of eggplant, grapes and fireworks.

FRANK THE WEATHERMAN
by First Graders

Every morning the children at Laurel Elementary School watched Frank the Weatherman on TV-21. Frank was a very mixed-up weatherman. When he predicted the weather, he was always wrong.

Everyone started to think that Frank didn't know how to predict the weather. They were even starting to think about watching another weatherman on a different channel. Frank heard about this and was very sad.

So, Frank tried harder to predict the weather, but the opposite of what he said would happen. If he said it was going to be sunny, it would rain. If he said it was going to be hot, it would be cold. The boys and girls never knew what to wear to school.

So, the boys and girls sent Frank an e-mail. It said:

> *Dear Frank,*
> *We like you, but your predictions are crazy. Maybe you forgot to plug in your radar and satellite. You need your storm tracker!*
>
> *Love,*
> *Your Friends at Laurel Elementary*

When Frank got the e-mail, he checked the radar plug. He said, "The students were right, I did forget to plug it in!" The next morning on TV, he predicted it was going to be sunny and guess what? It was sunny! The following day he said it was going to rain, and it did rain. From that day forward, everyone was happy with Frank's forecast.

Frank predicted the weather correctly every day. He wanted to thank the students for all of their help, so he decided to visit them. On the morning of his visit, Frank drove in the rain. When he reached the school, the rain stopped. When he got out of his car, the sun came out and he saw a beautiful rainbow over the school. Frank thought, "Wow! Laurel Elementary is a special place!"

A RAINBOW ACROSTIC
by First Graders

Ribbons of color

Amazing

Imagine

New

Beautiful and brilliant

Over our school

Wow!

THE TREASURE AT THE END OF MY RAINBOW

by Second Grader - Colton Brown

If I could find hope and joy at the end of the rainbow,

I would share it with everyone.

I would let everyone know to never give up and to keep trying.

I would remind them that God is always beside you.

I hope that everyone will help others in need.

We should all try to make other peoples' lives more joyful.

Life would be so great if that would happen.

RAINBOWS REMIND ME OF . . .

by Second Graders

A red crab,
        Grabbing with its sharp claws,
                Crawling on the beach.

An orange butterfly,
        Landing on a flower,
                Sipping nectar.

A yellow chick,
        Peeping loudly,
                Crying for its mama.

A green apple,
        Eating its sweetness,
                Tasting delicious.

Blue water,
        Falling down the waterfall,
                Talking to the trees.

An indigo flower,
        Blooming in the summer,
                Looking quite lovely.

A violet crayon,
        Waiting to be chosen,
                Drawing purple grapes.

How the Rainbow Got in the Sky
by Third Grader - Emily Gibson

Long, long ago, there lived a giraffe. Every day it rained, the giraffe would wear a colorful tie to cheer himself up.

One day, he had an idea to make a big tie of many colors. Every time it rained, he would put it on so that everyone could see it and share the colors with him.

It did not turn out to look like an ordinary tie. One day it rained and the tie got soaked and didn't dry up quite right. Instead of drooping down straight from his long neck, it looked more like a half of a circle.

Being the good natured giraffe that he was, he did not throw away his damaged tie. Instead, he gave his new creation a name. He called it a "rainbow," in honor of the rain that created it. He thought that would be the perfect thing to cheer people up when it rained.

Everyone loved it! So, every time it rains the giraffe holds the rainbow up so everyone can see it. Now, he doesn't even mind getting wet.

PIECES OF A PRISM
by Third Graders

Hearts, apples, roses, are all red, it's said.
Happy, loving feelings flow through my head.

Oranges are my favorite, a very tasty treat.
Peaches, pumpkins, tangerines, all are good to eat.

Yellow warms a room, happy and sunny.
Yellow like the sun, lemons and honey.

A slimy, green frog by twilight we hear,
Crunchy, green apples are juicy all year.

Blue water flows down rivers and streams.
Raindrops on rooftops bringing daydreams.

Indigo the darkest, most mysterious indeed.
Dark crystals, deep oceans and mystical beads.

As lilacs and lupines and irises unfurl,
Violet can be seen all over the world.

RAINY WITH A CHANCE OF HOPE *by Fourth Graders*

It was a dark, gloomy morning in the little town of Hope. In the courtyard of Hope's little school, the fourth graders slowly walked into the building. Today was the dreaded fourth grade exam.

As the school day began, several of the fourth graders, particularly Cherie, George and Gavin had an uneasy feeling about the weather. As the 4th graders were about to begin their test, the lights suddenly went out. The class erupted, screaming in horror.

Standing by the window, George noticed someone standing outside in the thunderstorm. Timidly, George asked his teacher if he could go outside to help the stranger. The class couldn't believe it. They thought he was crazy to offer a stranger help. After much pleading, George finally convinced his teacher to let him help this man.

"You shouldn't talk to strangers," Miss Hart said to him, "but the storm really is quite dreadful. You can go, but not without an adult." She grabbed George's hand, and they walked out together.

As they reached the front of the school, they cautiously opened the front door, and there he stood. The man was soaking wet, his body was shivering and his feet were covered with mud. They led the man through the hallways, back to their classroom. When they arrived, Gavin fetched some paper towels for him. Cherie offered him her furry coat, which was way too small but kept him warm.

As the rest of the fourth graders gathered around the stranger, the electricity came back on. When the children looked closer, they realized the man was the new janitor, Mr. Fuzzy. He had left his keys inside his locker and locked himself out of the building.

As the children continued to help him dry off, the sun peeked through the clouds. The class felt a warmth from helping the new janitor. Mr. Fuzzy was also appreciative of all their support and kindness.

"Thank you, children," Mr. Fuzzy said in his heavy accent. He smiled at the class and then walked up to George. He quietly murmured, "Thank you for your love. Maybe there still is hope in this crazy world."

THE AUTOBIOGRAPHY OF A MUD PUDDLE
by Fourth Graders

A raptor was chased all over the place.
Two-thousand years later, there was no trace.
All that was left was a gigantic dent,
until the raindrops were finally sent.

Now the rain falls from the sky.
Sometimes I get water in my left eye.
I used to give drinks to a family of deer,
but now I only have bugs in my ear.

One day there was a yellow duck
that walked through me and he got stuck.
This duck is making my water turn black.
I wish that he would get off my back.

Now I have no use at all.
Everyone needed me throughout the fall.
I'm getting smaller by the day,
headed back to clouds turned gray.

I have reached a very old age.
This is my evaporation stage.
Now it's time to leave this place.
I will come back with a brand new face.

RAINBOW OF HOPE *by Fifth Graders*

As my mother Mata, my dad Kevaho, my brother Tomi, and my sister Naomi sat down to breakfast, I, Maui, wearily dragged myself out of bed and thought about the terrifying nightmare I had the night before.

I dreamed that a massive hurricane arose from the ocean and destroyed our beloved island of Vanuato. How could I tell my family and fellow villagers? How would they feel?

As I joined my family at the breakfast table, my Grandpa Pepe, the chief of the village, and Grandma Lily had arrived for a cup of coffee. I decided to tell them about my dream.

"I had one of those dreams that a hurricane would destroy our island," I began. My mom's face froze. My grandparents laughed. Daddy Kevaho said, "I believe my daughter. Her visions have come true before!"

Grandpa Pepe decided to warn the other villagers. He grabbed a chiseler, a carving tool, and carved a warning on a nearby tree which read, "Warning: Hurricane Bull Ring is approaching! Go to the Great Cave of Quazimo." As my grandpa finished with his warning, he heard the sounds of charging wildebeests, who were injuring many civilians in their path.

The wind started howling. It began to pick up speed and the next thing we knew, a giant tidal wave came crashing down on us. Soon, we were swimming in four feet of water.

As we struggled to stay afloat in the murky and salty water, Tomi felt something bite his leg. As he turned his body about in pain, Naomi shouted, "Water snake!"

The fangs had sunk into his leg. Grandpa Pepe and Daddy Kevaho swam him to shore and dragged him to higher ground. We all followed behind. Grandpa ripped off his shirt and wrapped it around Tomi's leg. Afterwards, the men of the family picked up Tomi and carried him towards the cave of Quazimo. Once we arrived at the cave, we found a shaman. He removed the venom from my brother and saved his life.

We were all relieved until my mother yelled, "Where's Grandma?" My father immediately went to look for her. Running through the violent and viscous rain, Daddy Kevaho heard a cry in the wilderness. He sprinted to what he hoped was Grandma Lily, but found instead a small child. As he sprinted back with the child, he heard another voice.

He ran quickly towards the sound and found Grandma pinned under a fallen tree. With all his might, he lifted the tree, and pulled Grandma out. Together, along with the small child, they headed back to the cave.

Along the way, Kevaho noticed a frantic woman. He approached her and asked, "Is this your child?" The woman gratefully nodded her head and thanked him vigorously.

In time, the storm began to die down, but the flooding continued. One of the villagers, an old wise man, suggested that we head for the levies to fix them and stop the flooding. Our family, along with some of the villagers journeyed to the levies for this task.

When we arrived there, some of the tribal leaders took off their shirts and filled them with sand. They stacked these sandbags against the levy along with rocks and mud. However, this did not stop the water. We then began to chop down trees to help control the rapidly flowing water. As we were finishing our work on the levy, a stream of color magically appeared out behind the dark gloomy clouds. It was a rainbow!

I don't know why, but when I looked around at all the villagers, I knew we all felt safe. We were given a sign from above, a ray of hope, telling us everything would be alright.

Through this devastating hurricane, I learned to believe in myself and my family. My family and I were lucky to be alive. We learned that in a crisis like this the key is to always stay calm, stay together, and know that there is always a rainbow ahead.

FROM THIS POINT ON

by Fifth Graders

Six years old, headed to school.
I dreaded that day.
I met the greatest of teachers then,
all my fears and tears were no more.
From that point on, school was okay.

Seven years old, made a sea horse for Dad,
I met Julie.
We were friends through thick and thin
and will be forever.
From that point on, I had a best friend.

Eight years old, wrote a paper
hoping to win so I can eat with the author.
When the teacher read my name,
that was a very proud moment.
From that point on, I knew I could be anything I wanted.

Nine years old, sat through science
I can't believe I have to do this bug board.
I take home a board and kill all the bugs,
and pray it's all over soon.
From that point on, I knew to fear this thing they call science.

Ten years old, wrote a poem
thinking of all that I would owe 'em.
My teachers were my friends,
and my friends were my teachers.
From this point on, I will always be proud to be a Spartan.

JACKIE & DELAINEY *by Sixth Grader - Jackie Schlemmer*

When Jackie was born, she was a very big baby. She was also very tall! She began school when she was five years old. That's when it all started!

Everyone would make fun of her because she was so tall. They would call her names like "Giraffe," and "Long Legs," and other rude names. She didn't even have any friends! Jackie would cry before she went to school because she didn't want to cry later and get teased.

The first day of first grade was horrible because it was a new school. All of the kids treated her like any other new kid, horribly! For the first half of first grade she did not have any friends.

One day, a small girl named Delainey asked her if she wanted to read a book with her. The problem Delainey had was that the book she wanted to read was on the top shelf in the class. Delainey was very short and could not reach it. Jackie, being so tall, was easily able to retrieve the book, and they read it together. Jackie found out that Delainey understood what it was like to be teased because she was very short. Everyone teased her, too. After that day, they became best friends.

Jackie has a bunch of friends now. She uses her long legs to play basketball for her college basketball team. She is also successful in school. She still gets teased sometimes, but she doesn't let it bother her much anymore. Jackie knows that what is important in life is who you are and not what you look like.

Oh yeah, Delainey is doing well also. She is in college, too, and they remain the best of friends.

28

LIFE IS A RAINBOW
by Sixth Graders

Life is a rainbow
> With ups and downs
>> smiles and frowns

Life is a rainbow
> Each stripe
>> a different step in life.

Life is a rainbow
> Full of colors
>> a full range of emotions

Life is a rainbow
> Before you reach it
>> it fades away.

Life is a rainbow
> You endure the rain
>> to get to the sun.

WRITTEN WITH THE SUPPORT OF VUTHY KUON AND THE FOLLOWING STAFF:

Elementary Principal	Dennis Devorick
Kindergarten	Leigh-Ann Canciello, Carrie Mason, Nadine Mezan
First Grade	Melissa Armstrong, Mary Lou Boben, Jennifer Changoway, Rosemary Chmura, Todd Cole, Blanche Stach
Second Grade	Betty Bartolomeo, Jennifer Boyles, Kim Carlson Candice McCormick, Patricia Panek, Sherry Stambaugh
Third Grade	Kathy Atwell, Paula Kaldy, Gina Santini Cathy Staph, Christina Thakar
Fourth Grade	Helen Bowden, Deborah Haney, Bethany Kwiat Brenda McKissick, Michele Mrozek
Fifth Grade	Michelle Bowden, Wende Litrenta, Kristen Murphy, Patrick Silhanek, Mary Jo Wilson
Sixth Grade	Kevin Mahoney, Deborah McMillin, Angela Traggiai, Amanda Wade, Betsy Wolford
Specials	Maureen Daugherty, Pat Cuba, Jesse Croach, Pam Croach, Kristen Franus, Garrett Musko, James Marcantino
Title 1	Michelle Ault, Carey Cower, Jennifer Hileman, Stephanie Hennon, Rachel Sauders
Special Education Supervisor	Toni Mild
Special Education	Rhonda Hockenberry, Sarah Marcotullio, Kimberly McCabe, Denise Moccia, Robin Prossen, Jennifer Pezzuolo, David Spalding, Melissa Weatherby
AmeriCorps	Jodi Disman, Sarah Thompson, Meghan Wilson
Other Staff	Mike Czubiak, Daniel Fazzone, Debra Garrett, Heather McKissick, Paula Vogler
Secretaries	Kathy Palladino, Jessica Polivka, Sharon Marshall
High School Principals	Harold Dunn, Mike Krol
High School Art	Susan Gryn
High School Art Students	Erik Short, Nick Pisor
The Laurel Board of Education	Alan Carlson, Christopher Donegan, Blaine Forbes, Jeff Hammerschmidt, Cheryl McKee, Timothy Redfoot, David Smith, Earl Williams, Michael Zubasic
Superintendent	Dr. Sandra Hennon Mr. Leonard Rich Parents/Guardians of all our Students